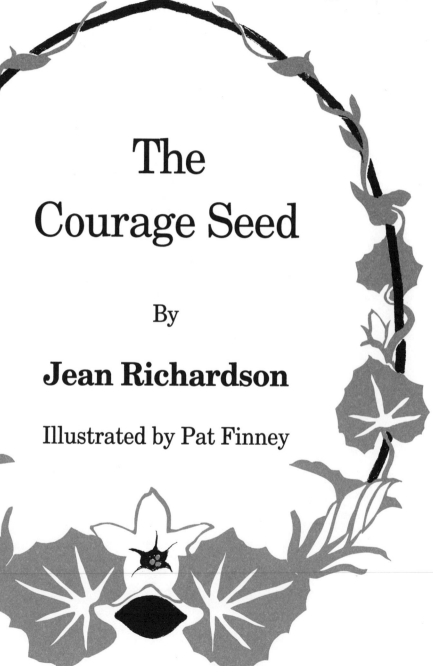

The
Courage Seed

By

Jean Richardson

Illustrated by Pat Finney

This book is dedicated to my Navajo students at
Valley Elementary School in Shiprock, New Mexico,
and to children everywhere who are struggling for
the courage to hold on to tradition while longing
to be accepted in a rapidly changing world.

Acknowledgments

Jean Richardson and Pat Finney would like to thank all the students and faculty at Valley Elementary School in Shiprock, New Mexico, and Townewest Elementary in Houston, Texas, for their support and co-operation. Special gratitude goes to the following people, whose names, faces, and/or stories were used in this book:

Ramzi Abilmona
Renee Boyd
Christopher Cherry
Andrea Cifuentes
Mrs. Josie Damian
Tina Gonzales
Jessica Jackson
April Kelly
Mrs. Sara Lasater
Kimberly Le
Mary Manygoats
Christopher Newton
John Onwachekwa
Rishi Patel
Jason Reid
Mrs. Barbie Roth
Edward Shin
Abi Thomas
Inez Ventura
Tyler White

Mary Manygoats was too sick to go to school. She pulled the pillow down over her head to try to block out the sound of Aunt Betsy calling to her: "Get up! Don't be late for school on your first day!"

She raised the pillow just a crack to peek out at her strange, new room. Everything was starkly clean. The walls, floors, and ceiling all seemed untouched by human hands. Even her brand new panda bear, sitting alone in the small rocker, seemed too clean to touch.

Mary looked at the calendar on the wall above the panda. The picture on the calendar showed the space shuttle sitting on a launch pad. She liked that picture. It made her think of home. She studied it carefully, trying to decide why it looked so familiar. Then she remembered. It looked very much like the giant rock near her home in New Mexico, the one white man called "Shiprock."

Mary tried to remember the Navajo name and story behind the huge rock. Did her grandfather, Night Singer, say that it was the giant butterfly that had carried her ancestors to that country on its wings? She wished now she had paid more attention to his stories. Just thinking about her grandfather made her start to cry.

1

"**M**ary! Mary—are you up yet?"

"No." Mary tried to shut out the starkness of the room. How she missed her familiar hogan with its warm, sandy floor. She missed the smell of dinner cooking on the big, black stove in the center of the room. She thought about the summer hogan, just a shelter made of sticks and branches, where they all slept outside in hot weather. In those days, when she couldn't sleep, she could watch the incredible, ever-changing star show in the heavens. Grandfather, of course, could tell wonderful stories about the stars.

Mary's favorite story was how First Woman mixed up the stars. Mary remembered that First Woman and First Man created the sun out of clear stone. Then they carved the moon out of a piece of crystal. Next, First Man gathered pieces of sparkling mica for the stars. He laid them out in pleasing patterns, such as the Big Dipper, on the hogan floor. Then First Man became sleepy and lay down for a nap. First Woman, tired of all the clutter on the hogan floor, gathered up the remaining pieces of mica and threw them upward. They scattered all over the sky.

First Man was quite angry when he saw what First Woman had done. "Someday," he said, "I must rearrange them into a more pleasing pattern." But somehow he never had the time. The stars have remained scattered in the sky, waiting to be properly placed.

Mary looked up at the bright, electric light over her bed and began to cry again.

"Hurry up. You'll be late for school!" Aunt Betsy called.

"I'm not going!"

"You most certainly are!" Aunt Betsy swished into the room and yanked back the covers. Even Aunt Betsy was squeaky clean—from her carefully combed hair to her neatly polished shoes.

Mary rolled slowly over onto her stomach and stretched her right leg down until her big toe was just touching the floor. Using every muscle in her body, she lifted herself to a standing position. Then, as if moving to a distant drumbeat, she marched slowly to the closet. The vivid colors of her new clothes seemed to shout at her. Covering her eyes with her hands, she sank down in the corner of the closet and began to remember.

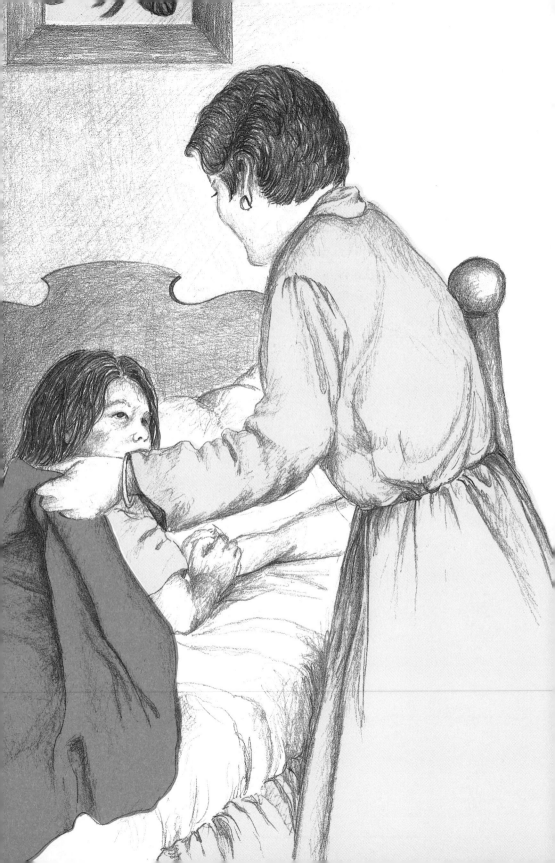

The distant drumbeat was louder now. Slowly, slowly . . . a funeral pace. She marched along, straight and tall. Alone, all alone, the last living member of her entire family.

Mary heard the voices again, as clearly as if they were in the closet with her.

"Such a terrible tragedy. Her whole family killed in an auto accident. They were on the way home after leaving Mary at the boarding school in Shiprock. Who will care for her now, the poor little thing?"

"I understand that she has an aunt Betsy who teaches in Houston. Betsy has agreed to take Mary back to Texas with her. It's so sad . . . sad . . . sad . . ."

Mary flung out her arms to push the voices away. Her hand hit a big bag of something soft. It was her old "Indian" clothes that Aunt Betsy was planning to donate to charity.

"You must put all the old things behind you, now that you have started a new life in the city," Aunt Betsy had said.

Mary felt around until she found her favorite purple skirt and pink blouse that her grandmother had made for her. The material was soft from many washings and the colors had faded, but she felt better as soon as she put them on.

She dug deeper to see what else the sack might contain. There was something hard and lumpy in the very bottom. Her heart jumped as soon as her fingers closed on it. She didn't even have to look to see what it was. She put the necklace over her head and ran her fingers lovingly over each piece of turquoise.

T urquoise, Grandfather had said, was a gift of the gods. On clear mornings, he used to tell her, the Bearer of the Sun rode forth on a turquoise-colored horse.

Mary knew that these were the stones Grandfather had collected as a young man from the secret place that his own grandfather had shown him. He had strung the pieces together as a token of his love for her grandmother, Dawn Woman, many years ago.

How could Aunt Betsy possibly have wanted to throw away something so precious?

Then Mary remembered something her grandmother once told her. "Never cut your hair," Dawn Woman had said as she lovingly stroked Mary's long hair with her special brush. "The memory of all the stories of our people is stored in your hair. If you cut it off, you will forget all those wonderful things that are special to the Navajo."

Mary turned and strode defiantly into the kitchen.

"Well, I see you're finally ready."

Aunt Betsy gave her a disapproving look. "No time to change your clothes. I guess you'll just have to go like that."

Mary stared briefly at Aunt Betsy's short hair. Now she understood how Aunt Betsy could forget her Navajo ways so easily. She turned and hurried out the door before her aunt could change her mind.

As she walked along, Mary began to sing her mother's favorite chant:

> *May it be beautiful before me,*
> *May it be beautiful behind me,*
> *May it be beautiful below me,*
> *May it be beautiful above me,*
> *May it be beautiful all around me.*

But as she got closer to the school, she walked slower and slower. Mary began noticing the other girls waiting on the playground for the doors to open. They all seemed to be dressed in their Sunday best. Why on earth had she worn these old funny-looking clothes after Aunt Betsy had bought her all those nice new ones? Mary stood behind a big oak tree and tried to become invisible.

Finally everyone went into the school. Clutching her necklace with one hand for courage, Mary approached the big doors with dread. Would anyone talk to her? Would they make fun of her and laugh at her Indian clothes? She looked so different. She felt like the black sheep in her grandmother's flock of fluffy white lambs.

Suddenly, an arm came around her shoulders and a kind, motherly voice spoke to her.

"Would you like some help finding your classroom?" The voice belonged to a tall, friendly-looking woman. "I'll bet I can guess your name. Is it Mary Manygoats?"

Mary looked at the woman in disbelief. "How did you know my name?" she asked.

"It's very simple," the woman replied. "I'm Mrs. Lasater, the principal of this school. I knew you would be coming today, so I was expecting you.

"Oh my," she said, looking at her watch. "We'd better hurry or you'll be late." She gently led Mary down the hall and into a classroom.

"Mrs. Williams, here is another new student for you," Mrs. Lasater said in a loud voice. "Her name is Mary Manygoats."

Mrs. Williams was a cheerful, young teacher with a happy smile and lots of curly, brown hair. She hurried across the room toward Mary.

"Welcome! You're just in time. Please take a seat so we can get started."

Mary had already spotted a vacant chair in the far corner of the room, so she headed in that direction. She walked hurriedly through the sea of curious eyes and sank down in the chair, still clutching her necklace tightly. The teacher began talking again, and one by one the faces turned back toward the front of the classroom. Mary let out a tiny sigh of relief.

"Students, since today is the first day for everyone, I think we should each introduce ourselves. My name is Mrs. Williams and I am happy to be your teacher this year. I am married and have a three-year-old son named Mike. My husband is studying to be a doctor. My favorite game is Trivial Pursuit, and I collect rocks. Now that you know all about me, I'd like to know more about each of you. Let's start here on the front row, and each of you can tell the class about yourself."

Mary, who had just started breathing deeply again, was stunned by this announcement. She shrank down in her chair until her neck rested on the cold metal of the chair back and her knees bumped the underside of her desk. How could she stand up and have them all laugh at her?

A small girl sitting on the front row nearest the door was the first to speak. Mary couldn't hear a word the girl was saying because her own heart was pounding in her ears. Several students stood up, one at a time, before Mary could quiet her thumping heart enough to hear. How she longed to be back at the Navajo school with the friends she had known all her life. At that school, only the teachers were strangers.

Mary began to wonder what she would say when it was her turn. How could she explain why she looked so different? She didn't have any hobbies, unless herding the Churro sheep could be called a hobby. Perhaps if she listened closely, she could get some ideas from the other students.

A tall boy named Rishi was telling about the home he remembered in India. He described in great detail a beautiful palace he had visited in the city of Agra. As Mary listened, she imagined that she could see the Taj Mahal shimmering above his head.

Next a girl from Colombia told about the home she hadn't seen since she was small. She spoke of the cobblestone streets and the wrought-iron balconies on the buildings. But especially she remembered the wild orchids. Mary could almost smell the sweet fragrance of the blossoms as the girl talked.

When the teacher called "Chris," two boys jumped up. They were both named Chris, and they were both from England. They looked enough alike to be brothers. They had met out on the playground and already were friends.

The two boys took turns telling about their favorite places in London, where they both were born. They talked about Big Ben, the largest bell in the Clock Tower of the Houses of Parliament. They described Trafalgar Square, Charing Cross, the Tower of London, and Piccadilly Circus. When they were finished, everyone wanted to go to London.

April, a small girl with dark brown hair braided in tiny cornrows, was next. She was from the island of Jamaica. She told of the city houses where her aunts and cousins lived, but mostly she remembered life on her grandmother's farm.

She talked about the chickens, goats, and pigs her grandmother raised. She remembered the colorful flowers that grew near their home in the Blue Mountains. In vivid detail she described the tall hibiscus plants with their pink and white blossoms. She missed all those things, but most of all she missed her grandmother.

Jason, a boy from the Philippines, came after April. He described his home on stilts, the long front porch, and the swaying palm trees all around his house. He said the family used sleeping mats that were rolled up in a corner.

Jason also explained how the carabao, or water buffalo, did most of the work in the rice fields. And he described the caramata, or two-wheeled cart, which was used to transport almost anything.

"But my caramata now is a bicycle," he said. "I'm going to be a famous bicycle racer when I grow up!"

The next student was a very blonde girl from the Netherlands.

"Some people call it Holland," she said, "but the real name, Netherlands, means 'the low countries.' And it *is* a low country. Most of our land was reclaimed from the sea by building dikes to keep the water out. We are most famous for our windmills and tulips. For special occasions we put on our lace caps and wooden shoes. I still have my wooden shoes. Maybe one day I could bring them to school."

The boy next to her stood up and pointed to his chest when it was his turn. "My name is Syngman, but my sister calls me 'Dragonfish' and my dad calls me 'Young Dragon.' We are Korean, but I do not remember Korea because I was born in America. I have seen pictures of the pagodas and the royal tombs at Kokuryo. Someday I would like to go there to visit."

"I have a funny name too," the next boy said. "I live in Pakistan, and my name is Iskander. You can call me 'Ike.' My parents are here on a grant from the university were my father teaches. We live in East Pakistan, which is flat country covered with bamboo, mango, coconut palm, and date palm trees. Our forests have leopards, bears, and tigers. We don't have to go to a zoo to see those animals."

T he next girl stood up and twirled around in her colorful, full skirt. "My mama let me wear this special dress for the first day of school," she said. "It's a dress I would wear in Mexico for fiesta. My favorite places in Mexico are the churches and the plazas. We visit our relatives often, but America is our home."

Ramzi was the next to speak. "My parents came from Lebanon many years ago. I've never been there, but I've seen pictures of the palaces, with their high arches and the thick stone walls for shade. My favorite shirt is a Mickey Mouse T-shirt because we are going to DisneyWorld at vacation time. I think DisneyWorld must be the most wonderful place on earth."

The next girl's name was Kimberly. "My grandparents fled Viet Nam in a small sampan after the war. Sometimes they talk about the houses with thatched roofs and the flowers that grew wild. But I don't know of those things. I'm an American."

Tyler said, "I'm an American too. My ancestors came here from Ireland many years ago. I've never been there, but I've heard about the 100-year-old cottages with thatched roofs. Some people call it the 'Emerald Isle' because it's so green."

"My name is John and I'm from Nigeria," said the next boy. "I'm wearing a tie-dyed shirt that my aunt made especially for me. It has a Nigerian design."

"My name is Abi, and I'm from Nigeria too," said the boy across the aisle. "Many people think of Nigeria as a poor country, but we also have modern cities there. We have many of the same things as an American city."

Mary began to look around the room with more interest. These were certainly not the classmates she had expected. She began to wonder: What does a real American look like? Did anyone here really look like the children she had seen on Aunt Betsy's TV set?

The girl sitting next to her on the right was pretty enough to be on television. She had long, blonde hair and beautiful, blue eyes. Her expensive clothes made her look like an advertisement for a department store. Mary thought that if she only looked like that girl, her problems would be over.

The blonde girl's name was Jessica. She told the class about her father, who worked at NASA. She talked about a trip she had made to Florida to watch a shuttle launch.

But Mary wasn't listening. A tiny tear trickled down her face and landed on the desk silently. At that very moment she heard the teacher call her name.

"Mary, you are last. But I'm sure you have some interesting things to tell us."

In the silence that followed, Mary thought of something her grandfather once told her. "You can be brave," he told her when she was very small and had been afraid of the dark. "Look in your mind for the tiny seed of courage."

"Do I have seeds in my mind?" Mary had asked.

"Everyone does," Grandfather replied. "The seeds for love, hope, and courage are all there. But they will never grow big and strong unless you tend them well. Brave deeds help the courage plant grow strong, just as rain helps plants in the desert."

Mary took a deep breath and stood up. "My name is Mary Manygoats," she said. Mary was surprised by the clear, calm sound of her own voice. "I am a Navajo from Shiprock, New Mexico."

Every head in the room turned and looked curiously in her direction. Mary bravely continued. "My grandfather, Night Singer, was a shaman and a great storyteller of the Dineh, our people. My grandmother, Dawn Woman, was famous for the beautiful patterns and brilliant colors in the blankets she wove. My old hobby was herding Churro sheep, but now I have to find a new hobby."

"Thank you, Mary," the teacher said when Mary quit speaking. But Mary did not sit down. Looking all around the room at the expectant faces, she smiled shyly.

"On behalf of my entire tribe," she said in a voice that sounded very much like her grandfather's, "I'd like to welcome all of you to America."

WHERE IN THE WORLD DID THEY COME FROM:

1. INDIA
2. COLOMBIA
3. ENGLAND
4. JAMAICA
5. PHILLIPINES

6. NETHERLANDS
7. KOREA
8. PAKISTAN
9. MEXICO
10. LEBANON

11. VIET NAM
12. IRELAND
13. NIGERIA
14. TEXAS
15. NEW MEXICO

Native American Face Painting

WORDS

How to Say Them and What They Mean

Anasazi (ana-soz´-ee): The ancient ancestors of the Navajo.

Churro (chur´-ro): Type of sheep herded by the Navajo.

Crystal (krist´-l): A clear, colorless mineral.

Dineh (dee´-ney): Name that the Gods gave the Navajo; it means "the people."

Dinetaa (dee-ney-tah´): Land of the Navajo.

Hatali (ha-tal´-ee): A medicine man or chanter who was necessary for the "sings."

Hogan (ho-gahn´): An earth-covered, six-sided Navajo home.

Mica (mi´-ka): A shiny, transparent mineral.

Navajo (nahv´-ah-ho): The English name for the Indian tribe; it means "planters of huge fields."

Shaman (shah´-man): Navajo medicine man.

Sing (sing´): Navajo ceremony performed by a medicine man, usually for healing or to bring rain.

Turquoise (tur´-koiz): A blue-green mineral used by the Navajo for jewelry.

How God Created the Horse

In their legends the Navajo say God created the
horse in this way:

> *The horse was created of the dawn —*
> > *white and the black.*
> *His heart was made of red stone,*
> *Of lightning his ears,*
> *Of twinkling stars his eyes,*
> *Of white shell his teeth,*
> *Of beads his lips.*
> *His tail was made of black rain.*
> *His feet they made of a cloud;*
> *His gait, of a rainbow,*
> *And his bridle, of sun strings.*

Sand Painting

Sand Paintings

The most powerful healing rite was the sand painting, which was begun at sunrise and destroyed at sundown. The gods were the first makers of these paintings, and they drew them upon the black clouds.

The gods told man that he could make the magic paintings on the ground. Colored rocks and minerals of the desert were ground into fine powder. Then the one who had the right to carry out this sacred duty spread the clean sand upon the floor of the medicine hogan. From his bark trays of color, a small bit of the sacred powder was trickled between his fingers to make the fine lines and details of the painting. Usually this took hours of careful work.

The drawings contained forms of the gods, lightning, the rainbow, clouds, and other objects with spiritual meaning. These paintings were made only in the winter. Every year the painting had to be the same. It was the medicine man's responsibility to remember them exactly from winter to winter.

In the healing ceremony, the person to be cured was placed in the center of the picture, and the chanting and rituals began. An ill person could take a small portion of the sacred painting and share in its power. After the ceremony, powdered rock and golden sand were returned to their original spots in the desert.

Native American Symbols

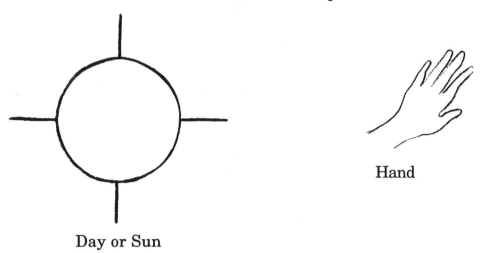

Day or Sun

Hand

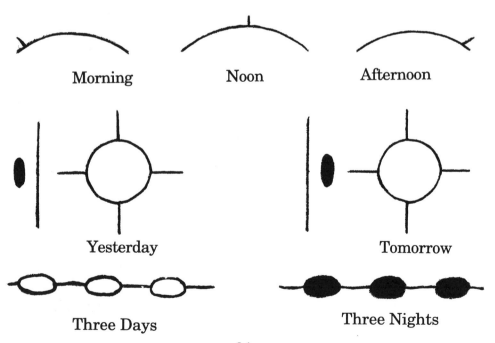

Morning

Noon

Afternoon

Yesterday

Tomorrow

Three Days

Three Nights

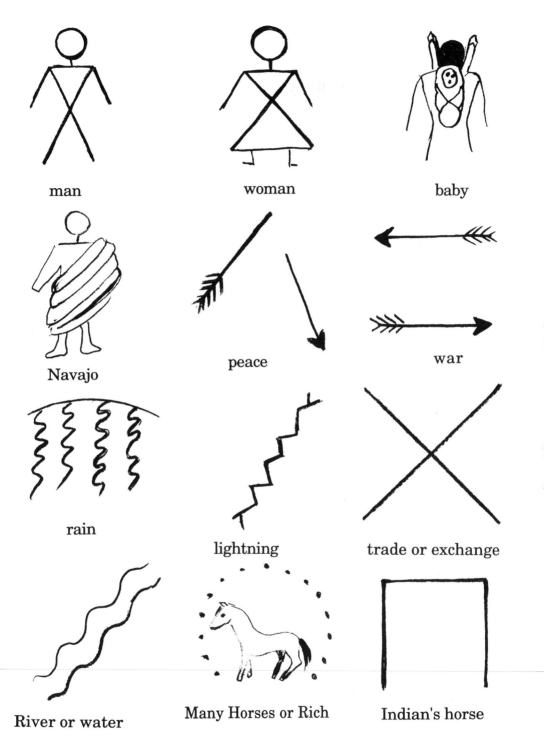

man

woman

baby

Navajo

peace

war

rain

lightning

trade or exchange

River or water

Many Horses or Rich

Indian's horse

Some Navajo Beliefs

Nothing man-made should be perfect, so a small mistake is
always woven into each rug.

Trees struck by lightning should be avoided.

We live in the "Fifth World of White Brightness."

Never kill a snake.

Never eat raw meat.

Never step over a sleeping person.

A man should never speak to his mother-in-law.

Hogans should always face the rising sun.

If someone dies in a hogan, it must be abandoned along
with everything inside it.

Corn has sacred properties. Legends say the gods created
the ancestors of the Navajo out of ears of corn.

Some Navajo Chants

Prayer to Spirits for Inspiration:

May it be beautiful before me,
May it be beautiful behind me,
May it be beautiful below me,
May it be beautiful above me,
May it be beautiful all around me.

Navajo Man's Chant to Dedicate Outside of New Hogan:

May it be delightful in my hogan,
From my head may it be delightful
To my feet may it be delightful,
Where I lie may it be delightful,
All about me may it be delightful.

Navajo Woman's Chant to Dedicate Inside of New Hogan:

May it be delightful, my fire,
May it be delightful for my children.
May all be well.
May it be delightful with my food and theirs.
May all be well,
May all of mine be well,
All my flocks, may they be well.

Chant for Healing

Happily I recover
Happily my interior becomes cool
Happily my eyes regain their power
Happily my head becomes cool
Happily my legs regain their power
Happily I hear again
Happily for me the spell is taken off
Happily may I walk
In beauty I walk.

To Learn More About
Native Americans

Amon, Aline. *Talking Hands*. New York: Doubleday & Co., 1968.

Bleeker, Sonia. *The Navajo*. New York: William Morrow, 1967.

Bureau of Indian Affairs. *Here Come the Navaho*. Tucson, Arizona: Treasure Chest Publications, 1953.

Erodes, Richard. *The Native Americans: The Navajos*. New York: Sterling Publishing, 1979.

Erodes, Richard. *The Pueblo Indians*. New York: Funk & Wagnalls, 1967.

Forman, Werner. *The Indians of the Great Plains*. New York: William Morrow, 1982.

Gridley, Marion E. *Indian Tribes of America*. New York: Rand McNally, 1973.

Helfman, Elizabeth S. *Signs and Symbols Around the World*. New York: Lothrop, Lee & Shepard Co., 1967.

Hunt, W. Ben. *Indian Crafts and Lore*. New York: Golden Press, 1954.

McGaw, Jessie Brewer. *How Medicine Man Cured Paleface Woman*. New York: William R. Scott, 1976.

70

ABOUT THE AUTHOR

A native Texan, Jean Richardson holds a B.S. degree in elementary education from the University of Texas at Austin and has taught school in seven states. She is the mother of three children and is active in several writing groups in Houston, where she now resides. Her first two books, *Tag-Along Timothy Tours Alaska* and *Tag-Along Timothy Tours Texas,* were written with the goal of teaching geography in an interesting and enjoyable manner. *Dino, The Dingbat Cat* is a book all in rhyme for fun, easy reading. The idea for *The Courage Seed* came from Jean's experiences teaching on the Navajo Reservation at Shiprock, New Mexico, and from the multi-ethnic diversity of her Houston classes. The characters in this book are based on real people. *The Courage Seed* is for all children who have ever been "outsiders."

ABOUT THE ILLUSTRATOR

The illustrations for this book were inspired by students in Pat Finney's art classes at Townewest Elementary in Sugar Land, Texas. Many of her students and their parents were born in other countries. Each student has woven his or her own customs into a cultural tapestry that provides a rich source of shared experiences, knowledge, and understanding.

Pat Finney has been interested in drawing and painting since she was a child. Her mother was an art teacher. Pat was born and reared in Fort Worth, Texas. She attended the University of Texas, North Texas State University, Texas Wesleyan University, and the University of Houston.

She has taught third, fourth, fifth, and sixth grades, as well as elementary and adult art classes. Her work has been exhibited in galleries at Taos, New Mexico, and at Fort Worth, Wimberley, and Houston, Texas. She lives and works in Sugar Land and Livingston, Texas.

71